D1613946

What I Tell Myself FIRST

Children's Real-World Affirmations of Self Esteem

Written by Michael A. Brown · Illustrated by Zoe Ranucci

This book is dedicated to...

Dedicated to **I Am That I Am**, who had a hand on my life and empowered me to charge forward regardless of the hurt. To Grandma Caroline, I love you, Nurse. Mommy, this book healed me. I get you now. I love you. Rest well, beautiful. (Tears) To Robert, Madison, Ava, and Amber-my children. Straight A's since pre-K. Your accomplishments never cease to amaze me. You are the fires in my rocket as I fuel your future. To those naysayers to what **I Am** had for me, you helped me learn that while no weapon formed against me shall prosper, I'll still be shot at and even hit. But, I'll survive. To those motivators through those sleepless nights in the fight for my kids, thank you. To Dan Lempa and Tommie Lott for the inspiration for the coloring and activity book that is to follow. Zoe, words cannot express the tears you made flow from this rock when I saw your work. Amazing. Your heart-soothing talent commands attention beyond your heart's desire. Thank you all. – MAB

Thanks to my friends and family who supported me along the way / To Mike for entrusting me your vision / Special thanks to Dustin for tagging me on Facebook and to my SCBWI group for your words of wisdom and guidance. – ZR

First Edition

Edited by Kendra Middleton Williams

Design and Illustration by Zoe Ranucci, www.GoodDharma.com

ISBN: 978-1-7341848-0-8

Library of Congress Control Number:2019917190

I am

_____

(Write your Name Here)

I am alive, alert, and able.
(Take a Deep Breath. Now, exhale.
Don't hold your breath, silly.)

3

The truth is

_____.

(What do you think the truth is?)

I must always tell myself the truth.

A lie is

_____ .

(What do you think a lie is?)

I must never lie to myself. EVER.

5

I must love me FIRST.

I must be selfish before I am selfless.

I am no-good to anyone else, if I am not good to myself.
I must do for myself, first. I must protect myself, first. 7

I am beautiful / handsome!

I will not be beautiful / handsome to everyone.
That is okay!
I am beautiful / handsome TO ME.

I like me!

Not everyone will like me.
That is okay! I like me!

My body is what it is.

Skinny, Fat, or Short with a Hat.
Tall, Small, Basketball!

I learn slow, so I will forget slow.

I am smart about what I know.

I can learn more. I will learn more.

I don't know everything.

I won't know everything. I want to be right.
But, I can't always be right.

If I am right, YAAAAYY!

If I'm not right, that's okay. I won't always be right.
Failure is a part of success if I learn from the failure.
What did I learn?

What I learned, I must teach another.

A sister from another mister
or a brother from another mother,
I can help others.

14

Change can be good. Change can be bad.

Change can be happy. Change can be sad.
I can change some things. I will change some things.
I won't change other things.

I am great at some things.

I am good at other things.

I am not good at some things.

I will perfect what I am good at doing.

I will work on what I am not good at doing.
I will either get better, or do something else.

Before I do anything, I must think first.

Two ears and one mouth.
Hear more with less mouth.

I must listen to plan.

I must listen to understand.
I must see beyond what is in front of me.

I must wait until the right time to do things.

I must speak when it's time.

I must speak what is mine.

It is NO ONE's job to
"Make Me" anything.
That is my job.

It is NO ONE's job to
"Heal Me" of anything.
That is my job.

It is NO ONE's job to **"Protect Me"** from anything.
That is my job.

21

I must make myself what I NEED to be to make myself what I want to be.

I must find what hurts me
to heal myself of what hurts me.

THREATS
BULLIES
PAIN
HURT

I must protect myself

by staying away from what hurts me.
I must stop what threatens me.
First, Fast, and Make it Last.

23

Work equals worth.

In my work, I am worth.
Respect is earned when I give respect.
I must act in a good way that earns respect.

How I look
can earn respect.

How I speak
can earn respect.

Not everyone will give me what I earn.
Not everyone will respect me. That is okay.

I respect me.

I am _____

(Write your Name Here)

I am alive, alert, and able.
(Take a Deep Breath. Now, exhale.)

Dear Reader,

I'm a dad like any other dad. I live for my children, and raising them into the best human beings they can be is my life's mission. The legacy I leave to the world is my children, and I'm like every other parent that wants their children to be strong, capable, productive, responsible, and most importantly, happy.

Having served my country in the Army, my community as a police officer, an anger management specialist, nonviolent crisis intervention instructor, and educator, I have learned a great many lessons. I hope to convey some of these lessons, as well as the real-world wisdom I've accumulated so far, to everyone that reads this book. I hope to teach a sense of self-love as well as self-acceptance. Giving a framework for both parents and children to help build their lives into sturdy and happy homes is my goal.

The ethos of any organization is a creed, oath, or promise to fulfill the values they stand for in their work. And I hope that this short ethos can, and I wish you well in the forging of your own personal ethos!

On the pages you will see places to fill in your name, choose adjectives that suit you personally, and answer short questions. These were put in place to not only personalize the book for each child individually, but to provoke meaningful discussions between the child and the parent. Of course, the parent may not be the only figure reading this book to a child, so please personalize it to suit your own relationship title with the recipient of the reading. No matter how you do it, it's exactly right for you, as long as it's true! So have fun, and happy reading!

Michael A. Brown

MASLOW'S HIERARCHY OF NEEDS

ABRAHAM MASLOW

SELF-ACTUALIZATION
MORALITY, CREATIVITY, SPONTANEITY, PROBLEM SOLVING, LACK OF PREJUDICE, ACCEPTANCE OF FACTS

ESTEEM
SELF-ESTEEM, CONFIDENCE, ACHIEVEMENT, RESPECT OF OTHERS, RESPECT BY OTHERS

LOVE/BELONGING
FRIENDSHIP, FAMILY, SEXUAL INTIMACY

SAFETY
SECURITY OF BODY, OF EMPLOYMENT, OF RESOURCES, OF MORALITY, OF THE FAMILY, OF HEALTH, OF PROPERTY

PHYSIOLOGICAL
BREATHING, FOOD, WATER, SEX, SLEEP, HOMEOSTASIS, EXCRETION

Abraham Harold Maslow (April 1, 1908 - June 8, 1970) was a psychologist who studied positive human qualities and the lives of exemplary people. In 1954, Maslow created the Hierarchy of Human Needs and expressed his theories in his book, Motivation and Personality.

Self-Actualization - A person's motivation to reach his or her full potential. As shown in Maslow's Hierarchy of Needs, a person's basic needs must be met before self-actualization can be achieved.

©Tim van de Vall

CPSIA information can be obtained
at www.ICGtesting.com
Printed in the USA
LVHW072229181119
637806LV00020B/194/P